Let's Roll

HOT RODS

by Wendy Hinote Lanier

FOCUS READERS

North Star EDITIONS

www.northstareditions.com

Produced for North Star Editions by Red Line Editorial.

Photographs ©: andykazie/iStockphoto, cover, 1; Kyser Lough/Murray Ledger & Times/AP Images, 4–5, 29; lembi/Shutterstock Images, 7; OweAnd/Shutterstock Images, 9; WGI/AP Images, 10–11; Brad Remy/Shutterstock Images, 13; littleny/Shutterstock Images, 15; Richard Thornton/Shutterstock Images, 16–17; Keith Bell/Shutterstock Images, 19; Chris Curtis/Shutterstock Images, 21; Jim Parkin/Hemera/Thinkstock, 22–23; Radoslaw Lecyk/Shutterstock Images, 25; Rick Donovan/iStockphoto, 26–27

ISBN
978-1-63517-049-8 (hardcover)
978-1-63517-105-1 (paperback)
978-1-63517-206-5 (ebook pdf)
978-1-63517-156-3 (hosted ebook)

Library of Congress Control Number: 2016951018

Printed in the United States of America
Mankato, MN
August, 2017

About the Author

Wendy Hinote Lanier is a native Texan and former elementary teacher who writes and speaks to children and adults on a variety of topics. She is the author of more than 20 books for children and young people. Some of her favorite people are dogs.

TABLE OF CONTENTS

FORD

CHAPTER 1

HOT ROD ROAD TRIP

It's a clear summer morning in June. The streets are suddenly packed with thousands of hot rods as the Hot Rod Power Tour takes to the open road. Hot rods are classic cars with large, powerful engines.

Drivers roll through Kentucky during the Hot Rod Power Tour.

The cars are following a route to seven US cities. It's the ultimate road trip.

At one stop, a crowd gathers around a vintage 1932 Ford Deuce

POWER TOUR

The Hot Rod Power Tour is an annual event that takes place in June. The seven-day tour covers seven cities and more than 1,500 miles (2,414 km). Approximately 2,000 hot rods are part of the tour, with more than 3,500 people completing the entire trip. The tour showcases many different makes and models of hot rods.

This hot rod's hood is open so people can get a closer look at the engine.

Coupe. The owner pops the old car's hood. Everyone admires the original Ford flathead V8 engine.

FUN FACT

People who own and work on hot rods are often called gearheads.

The owner turns the key, and the engine roars to life. The crowd shouts its approval over the noise.

On the road again, the hot rodders head to the next city on the tour. This evening's event is a car show and demonstrations by the Specialty Equipment Market Association (SEMA). Tomorrow's

Hot rod engines are sometimes taller than the hood of the car.

drive will take them to a new city and a special racing competition.

CHAPTER 2

HOT ROD HISTORY

The first hot rods were made during the 1930s. At that time, the **economy** was bad. Most people could not afford new cars. Soon people began restoring cars from junkyards.

Two men work on a hot rod in the 1950s.

People swapped out engines and searched the junkyards for parts. They created **streamlined** custom cars to race on straight-line courses. The dry lakebeds of southern California were perfect for these courses.

FUN FACT

In 1963, the Beach Boys released an entire album of songs about hot rods. Among them was "Little Deuce Coupe," a song about a 1932 Ford hot rod.

Some hot rod owners paint flames on their cars.

World War II (1939–1945) brought an end to hot rodding for a time. But when the war was over, interest in hot rods returned. Many soldiers had learned mechanical skills in the military.

They applied these skills to building faster cars. The popularity of hot rods grew. The first national Hot Rod **Exhibition** was held in 1948.

HOT WHEELS

For decades, children have enjoyed playing with hot rod toys. The Mattel company introduced the first Hot Wheels die-cast cars in 1968. Its first car was a blue 1968 Chevrolet Camaro. Since then, Mattel has sold more than one billion Hot Wheels vehicles.

Pony cars, such as this Chevrolet Camaro, are affordable but sporty.

In the 1950s, new kinds of hot rods included lowriders and custom show cars. Then, in the 1960s, muscle cars and pony cars were introduced. Hot rodding was here to stay.

Chapel
1923
Ford
Gray
GRANDPA

CHAPTER 3

THE MAKING OF A HOT ROD

Early hot rods were usually Ford Model A or Model T **roadsters** because they were plentiful and cheap. These common cars had no roof and only one seat.

This hot rod is based on a 1923 Ford Model T.

The hood, fenders, running boards, and windshield were all removed. Larger tires were installed on the back to raise the rear. Smaller tires on the front tilted the nose down. These changes helped increase speed and reduce wind resistance.

FUN FACT

***Hot Rod*, the first hot rodding magazine, was first published in 1948. It is still being published today.**

A Ford pickup truck's hood is opened to display the flathead V8 engine.

The engine for most hot rods was a Ford flathead V8. Ford began **mass-producing** the V8s in 1932, making them cheap and easy to find. It was also easy to make

MAKING A LIVING

Today, many people make their livings restoring or creating custom cars. They use the latest tools and technology to create works of art. These specialty cars can cost tens of thousands of dollars. Some specialty car builders are so well known that they have their own TV shows.

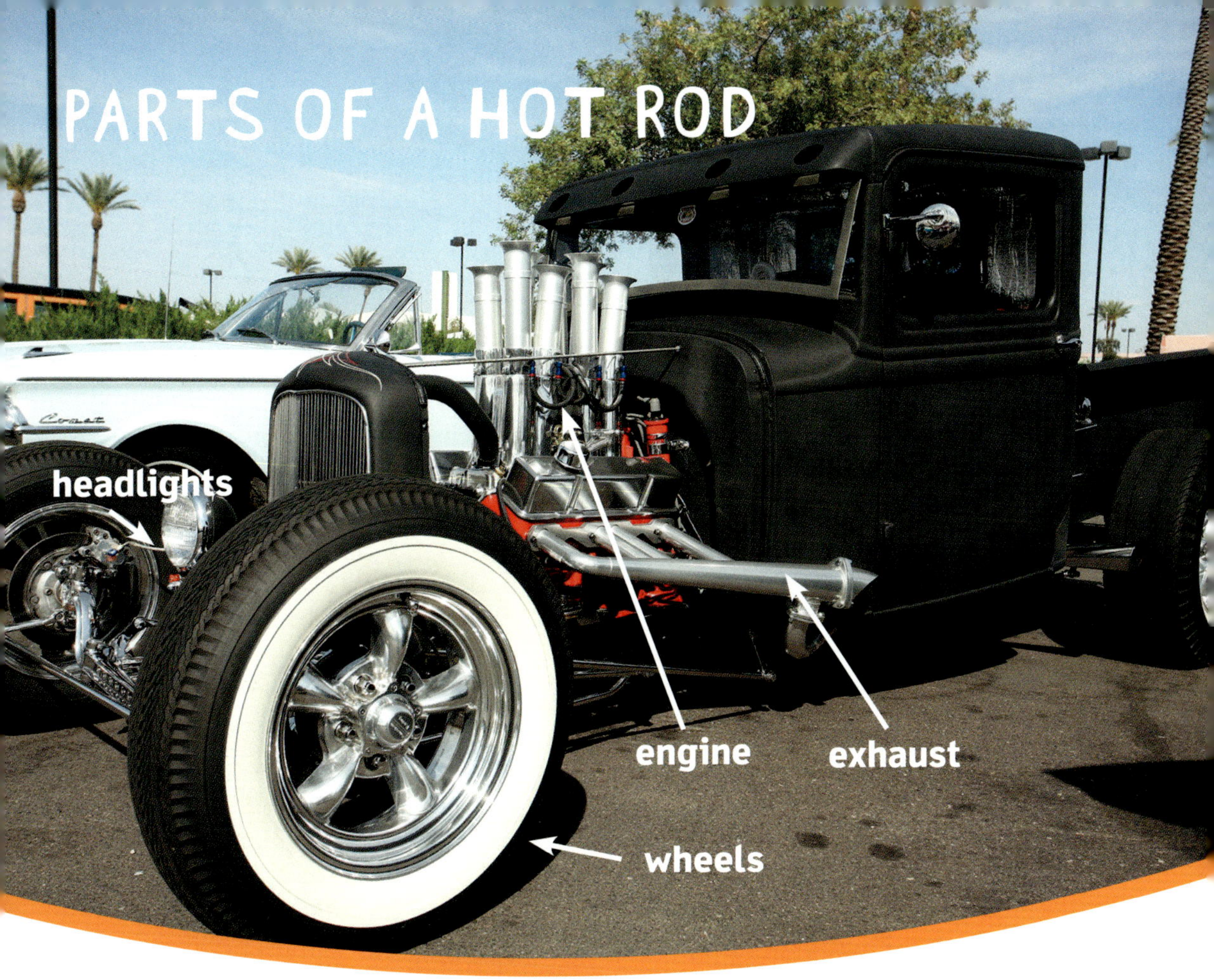

changes to boost performance. By changing out parts and making minor adjustments, hot rodders created engines that could go more than 100 miles per hour (161 km/h).

CHAPTER 4

TODAY'S HOT ROD

Hot rodding began as a way to bring new life to old cars. It allowed young people to own cars without spending a lot of money.

A car's artwork is as much a part of hot rodding as its engine.

But today's hot rods are part art and part mechanical wonder. And they are no longer cheap.

Hot rodding has become a big business. Companies make a wide variety of parts to "soup up," or customize, a **stock car**. They also produce newly made reproduction

FUN FACT

The first hot rod movies appeared in the 1950s. They included *Rebel Without a Cause* and *Thunder Road*.

A custom-built hot rod from the 1930s is on display at a car show in California.

parts that make it possible to build a complete hot rod. Hot rodding is a popular American pastime that is not likely to fade away.

HOW IT WORKS

CHRYSLER 426 HEMI

A popular engine for today's hot rods is the Chrysler 426 hemi. It gets its name from its combustion chambers, which are shaped like **hemispheres**. Its valves are in-line rather than side by side. The design allows for better airflow and less heat loss. This burns fuel more efficiently and wastes less energy. The spark plugs are centered at the top, providing more even ignition.

The first hemi engines were released in the early 1950s.

FOCUS ON

HOT RODS

Write your answers on a separate piece of paper.

1. Write a letter to a friend explaining the main ideas of this book.

2. Do you think it's a problem that hot rodding is no longer a cheap hobby? Why or why not?

3. When was the first national Hot Rod Exhibition held?

- **A.** 1932
- **B.** 1948
- **C.** 1968

4. Why might a hot rodder remove the car's running boards and windshield?

- **A.** to make the car go faster
- **B.** to make room for the engine
- **C.** to make the car's nose tilt down

5. What does **vintage** mean in this book?

A. old

B. expensive

C. crowded

At one stop, a crowd gathers around a **vintage** 1932 Ford Deuce Coupe. The owner pops the old car's hood.

6. What does **plentiful** mean in this book?

A. built without a roof

B. able to go fast

C. widely available

Early hot rods were usually Ford Model A or Model T roadsters because they were **plentiful** and cheap. These common cars had no roof and only one seat.

Answer key on page 32.

GLOSSARY

economy
A system of goods, services, money, and jobs.

exhibition
A public display of art or other items of interest.

hemispheres
Halves of a sphere.

mass-producing
Making goods in large quantities using machines.

roadsters
Early cars with open bodies, single seats, and large trunks or rumble seats.

stock car
A standard model of automobile.

streamlined
Specially shaped to reduce wind resistance.

TO LEARN MORE

BOOKS

Sandler, Michael. *Hot Hot Rods*. New York: Bearport Publishing, 2011.

Sodaro, Craig. *Blazing Hot Rods*. North Mankato, MN: Capstone Press, 2015.

Von Finn, Denny. *Hot Rods*. Minneapolis: Bellwether Media, 2009.

NOTE TO EDUCATORS

Visit **www.focusreaders.com** to find lesson plans, activities, links, and other resources related to this title.

INDEX

Answer Key: 1. Answers will vary; **2.** Answers will vary; **3.** B; **4.** A; **5.** A; **6.** C